To Sean
from
Aunt Shannon
&
Uncle Chip
1969

NIKOS
& THE SEA GOD

WRITTEN & ILLUSTRATED BY
HARDIE GRAMATKY

G. P. PUTNAM'S SONS   NEW YORK

Other books by Hardie Gramatky:

Little Toot

Bolivar

Hercules

Homer and the Circus Train

Sparky

Loopy

Creeper's Jeep

On an island far off the coast of Greece lives a boy named Nikos. He is a cheerful boy, a smile forever bursting forth on his sun baked face. His eyes reflect the blue of the sea.

Nikos lives with his old Aunt Mara in a house on the hillside. He has a pelican for a friend.

The island on which Nikos lives is a
lovely one. It is so small, though, that
ships passed by without noticing it.
Even the cruise ship from the mainland
sailed by each day without so much
as tooting a whistle.

The small island is all the world to Nikos.
The birds call and the seas roar and his little
world is a place for rejoicing.

Often he listened while Aunt Mara told him wonderful stories. Sitting each day under the vine leaves she told him about the Gods of Ancient Greece. She told about Zeus and Athena, and about Heracles and Poseidon.

She also told him of Pegasus, the wild, winged horse.

She told him of Icarus, whose wings were made of wax which melted when he flew too close to the sun.

Nikos spoke to his pet pelican. "I will call you Icarus, and you will be careful not to fly near the sun."

Sometimes Nikos went to the island's small museum and looked at the old vases.

There he found the mighty Zeus with his thunderbolt.

There was the beautiful and wise Goddess Athena. There, too, was the winged Nike, and the powerful Heracles.

One day at the far end of the museum Nikos came face to face with a picture of Poseidon, ancient God of the Sea. Here was an angry God who unchained the winds. Here was a violent God who stirred up storms at sea.

For a second—only a second—Nikos was sure that he saw a smile on the face of Poseidon. Then the smile was gone.

"This Poseidon is *endáxi*, this Poseidon is okay," Nikos said. He felt he had found a friend.

POSEIDON

From then on, whenever the weather was bright, Nikos would shout to Icarus: "Poseidon is friendly today! The sea is calm!"

But often in the nighttime, Nikos huddled under his blankets and heard the waves pounding against the island's rocky shore.

One night, when the winds howled and the sea roared, he knew that Poseidon was out there, stirring up the ocean, stirring up trouble, and when he looked through his window, he saw the dark form of the Sea God riding the waves.

The next morning Nikos told Aunt Mara the exciting news.

"Poseidon was out there last night!" he said.

Aunt Mara was all too ready to agree.

"He made the storm," Nikos said. "I heard him, and I saw him."

"And now he is taking a rest," said Aunt Mara, smiling.

Nikos hurried down a thousand steps to the public square to find the three old fishermen who spend their days sitting in the warm sunshine.

"Kalimera." Quickly Nikos said good morning.

"Kalimera to you," Andrea answered.

"I have news," Nikos said.

"Let us hear it then," said Androni.

"I saw Poseidon last night." Nikos said.

Andriko nodded his white beard. "When we sailed the seas, we saw him often. Isn't that so, Androni?"

"Certainly," said Androni. "He even said good morning to us. Isn't this so, Andrea?"

"Certainly," said Andrea. "But more often he tossed us around as if our boat were only a cork from a bottle."

The three seamen laughed together. And Nikos felt quite sure they had *never* seen Poseidon.

Each day, when the fishing boats put out to sea from the island, Nikos watched from the shore. When there was a storm he was glad, for then he knew he might see Poseidon again.

Sometimes Nikos and Icarus sailed out in their own small boat. Over and over he threw in his line. Over and over he pulled it back again, but he caught no fish. And never did he have so much as one glimpse of Poseidon.

Always Nikos came back without fish. And one day when his baskets were empty as usual, he saw Andriko and Andrea and Androni in the village square. They pounded their knees and laughed.

"Our young friend will never be a good fisherman," Andrea said.

"For no fish ever looks for his bait," Andriko said.

"We thought Poseidon was a friend of yours," said Androni.

"Maybe Poseidon is holding the fish by their tails," Nikos said. "Maybe tomorrow, he will let go—"

Sadly he went toward home. He hardly smelled the carnations that grew in the small gardens. He hardly saw the flaming red poppies that grew on the hills. He was afraid that Andrea was right. He would never be a good fisherman.

Aunt Mara came jogging along on the donkey, and she saw his empty baskets.

"Perhaps another day you will bring home a big catch of fish," she said. "It might even be that Poseidon will help you. Who can tell what will happen tomorrow?"

On the next day, Nikos sailed
out to sea, and again he threw in
his line. He remembered what
Aunt Mara had said. Perhaps this
would be the day he would take
home a fine catch. He felt a
hard tug on his line.

"It's a fish! It's a big one!"

He could hardly pull his line in
fast enough.

Then he saw what he had
caught. It was not a fish at all.
There on the end of his line was
an old Greek vase, as old as
the Gods themselves, perhaps.

Nikos was so angry that he started to throw the vase back into the sea. Then he saw a picture on it. It was a picture of Poseidon.

And Poseidon was holding a fish by the tail!

Nikos didn't know what to think.

Perhaps Poseidon wasn't his friend after all!

He shifted his sail for home, and as quickly as he reached shore, he rushed up the hill.

"What a strange catch," Andriko said.

"Almost as good as a fish!" said Androni.

The villagers came running to see what had happened.

"What bait do you use to catch a vase?" Andrea asked.

Aunt Mara threw up her hands. "It is a message from Poseidon, but what can it mean?" she said.

The sky was growing dark, and the old sails on the windmills turned faster and faster.

A storm was coming.

"Poseidon is coming for his vase!" Nikos yelled.

"Give Poseidon his vase," a villager called out.

Someone reached for it, and Aunt Mara's donkey kicked up his heels and Aunt Mara was sailing through the air.

The old women of the village clustered around Aunt Mara.

"She can speak," an old woman said, "but she cannot walk."

"I am sure that she has broken a leg," said another.

"If not two," said a third. "What shall we do?"

Nikos saw that no one knew what to do to help.

"We can get the doctor!" Nikos said.

"The doctor went to the mainland," said the third woman. "He will not return today."

Nikos thought of the cruise ship that passed the island each day. It would surely have a doctor aboard.

His friends the old seamen would help him. They would sail out and flag the cruise ship as it passed by.

"Will you help me, Andrea?" he asked. "Andriko? Androni?"

The seamen shook their heads. "It is not wise," Andriko said. "There is a storm at sea. Look. You cannot see where sky and water meet."

Nikos ran to his own small boat, and Icarus perched on the gunwhale.

"Come back, young friend," Andrea called.

But Nikos pushed his boat into the water and jumped in. He thought of the Sea God. "I am not afraid," he said to himself. "Poseidon will remember me."

They rode the pitching waves and the wind beat hard against them. Poseidon must be near, Nikos thought. And he is angry—

He watched through the mist and the spray. Surely Poseidon was there riding the tossing waves. He must be close, very, very close—

Nikos shivered with excitement.

The storm grew worse, and as Nikos watched through the gray black waves, he saw a dark form. "It *is* Poseidon. He is beating the waves into ugly gray foam." And Nikos was afraid.

The sea raged and the boat rocked. It was all Nikos could do to keep their little boat afloat.

The dark shape came close over the boat, and Nikos looked up. There was Poseidon. His beard was dripping wet, tangled with sea shells, but a smile was on his face.

Now a great wave seemed to lift the little boat high into the air. It was Poseidon himself lifting them, and Nikos and Icarus were safe.

When the winds calmed, Poseidon was gone with the storm.

Then Nikos saw the cruise ship. It was coming straight toward them. Nikos waved wildly while Icarus flapped his wings.

The Captain saw them, and in no time at all he lowered the boarding-ladder so that Nikos and Icarus could come aboard. And when he heard what had happened to Aunt Mara he quickly sent the ship's doctor ashore.

Aunt Mara was soon well, of course. Now visitors come to the island every day and she tells them her famous stories, always ending with, "And now I shall tell you about the time Nikos saw Poseidon, the God of the Sea."

And Nikos is a fine fisherman now. Andriko, Andrea and Androni will tell you this is so.

THE END